P9-AOD-438

Kingston Frontenac PL/ARPs

39011011796093

Feb 2017

The JOLLEY-ROGERS
and the
GHOSTLY
GALLEON

For Gran and Grandad:
for all the war stories and strong cuppas,
in front of the hottest fire in Salford.

Copyright © 2015 by Jonny Duddle

All rights reserved. No part of this book may be reproduced, transmitted,
or stored in an information retrieval system in any form or by any means,
graphic, electronic, or mechanical, including photocopying, taping, and
recording, without prior written permission from the publisher.

First published in the U.K. in 2015 by Templar Publishing
First U.S. edition 2016

Library of Congress Catalog Card Number pending
ISBN 978-0-7636-8910-0

16 17 18 19 20 21 BVG 10 9 8 7 6 5 4 3 2 1

Printed in Berryville, VA, U.S.A.

This book was typeset in IM FELL Double Pica and Tree Persimmon.
The illustrations were created digitally.

TEMPLAR BOOKS

an imprint of Candlewick Press
99 Dover Street
Somerville, Massachusetts 02144

www.candlewick.com

The JOLLEY-ROGERS and the GHOSTLY GALLEON

JONNY DUDDLE

templar books
an imprint of Candlewick Press

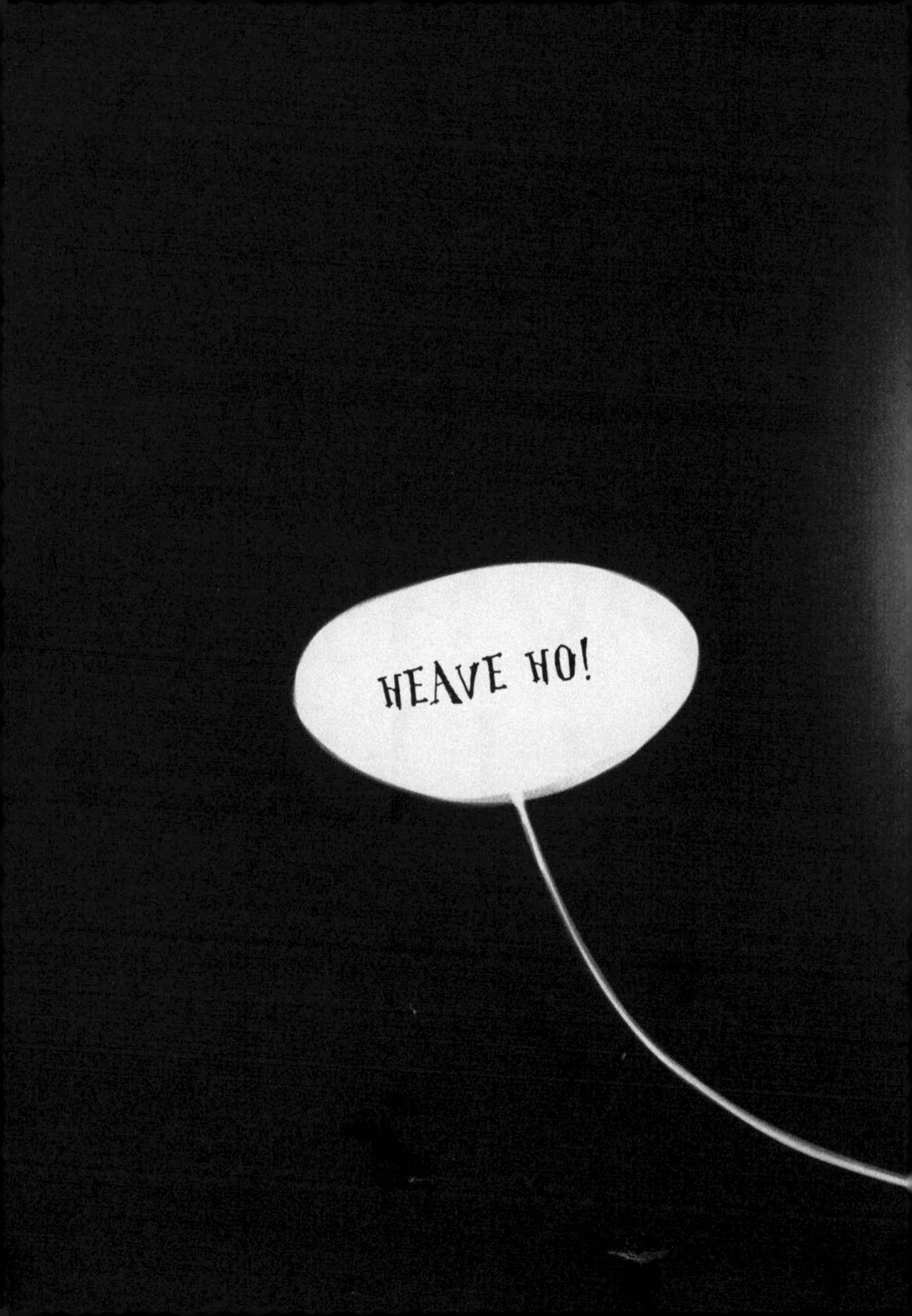
HEAVE HO!

Under the light of the moon we go!
We'll take yer silver, we'll take yer gold,
We'll take what we want to line our hold!
Some say we're cursed, some say we're dead!
We're in search of a key as you sleep in bed!

Heave ho! Heave ho!
Under the light of the moon we go!

CRUNCH!

The boat's keel smashed into the shore, plowing a deep furrow up the beach.

Heavy leather boots fell silently onto the sand.

Flintlocks were primed.
Daggers were drawn. Cold,
dead steel flashed in the
moonlight. A mass of dark briny
shadows surged across the beach and up
the steps, disappearing into the moonlit
alleyways of Dull-on-Sea.

1.
THE MUSEUM

Sitting in the cozy control room of the
Dull-on-Sea Museum, Arthur Poppycock
bit into his double-chocolate muffin and
slurped his coffee.

"Mmmm, how delicious,"
he mumbled as soggy crumbs
tumbled down his chin.

Being a security guard was the best job Arthur had ever had. Endless cups of coffee, as many muffins as he could eat (without Mrs. Poppycock reminding him of his pant-button problem), plenty of time to read *VW Beetle Monthly*, and hours of silence to tackle his beloved crosswords. *But best of all*, thought Arthur, *nothing EVER happens in Dull-on-Sea.*

CREAK!

"What was that?"

CLANK!

"Probably a cat in the alley," Arthur muttered. He switched to the alley camera, but there was nothing on the screen.

CLUNK!

"Or a very big mouse . . ."

CRASH!

"I'd better check," he told himself.

The only bad thing about his job at the Dull-on-Sea Museum, apart from the itchy sweater and having to polish his shoes every day, was that Arthur was a little bit afraid of the dark. Everything looked spooky beyond the glow of his flashlight. There were funny shadows everywhere: statues ... sculptures ... stuffed animals ... paintings ... and ...

2.
THE NEWS

"Good morning, this is Dull TV. Reports are coming in that the Dull-on-Sea Museum has been ransacked by pirates."

DULL TV

"Police say that the museum's camera failed to catch sight of the intruders, and no fingerprints or other evidence has been found. At this stage they only have the mumbled account of crossword champion and museum security guard Arthur Poppycock to go on.

"We now go live to the news conference at Dull-on-Sea police station, where Chief Inspector Klewless will be sharing the latest developments."

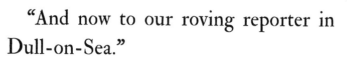

"And now to our roving reporter in Dull-on-Sea."

I was just walking home when I saw 'em. Hundreds of 'em, there were. Waving their cutlasses and singing and cursing and all excited. Carrying a load of treasure, they were. My wife didn't believe me. Said I was making things up, she did. Told me to sleep in the spare room and not to mess up the clean laundry, 'cause it was all neatly folded.

I'd been ironing all day. And now I'll have to wash the sheets. They smell like stale beer and fries, and we've got guests coming Tuesday. Pirates, he said. Have you ever heard anything like it? Pirates in this day and age?

"So, that's eyewitness Mervyn Wobley and his wife, Sheila, residents of Sea View Terrace. Now back to the studio."

Matilda munched on her Pirate Pops and listened to the radio intently.

"The robbery at the Dull-on-Sea Museum comes one month after the archaeological dig at Parrot Point was mysteriously ransacked in the night. Many of the treasures from the Parrot Point shipwreck had already been taken to the Dull-on-Sea Museum for safekeeping, but these were stolen in last night's raid. Police are yet to confirm that the two crimes are linked."

Matilda loved pirates. In fact, her best friend, Jim Lad, was a pirate. Taking an old bottle from the recycling box, she decided to write him a letter. If pirates were involved, maybe Jim would know something about it.

We would advise residents to lock up their valuables and not to answer the door late at night, particularly to pirates. But we would also remind you that pirates aren't generally a problem in Dull-on-Sea. Most important, DON'T PANIC!

DULL FM

3.
PANIC!

Though it had been almost a month since the robbery at the museum, Dull-on-Sea was still in a panic.

Now everybody seemed to be in a hurry. Shopkeepers shut their shops early. Police cars hurtled along with sirens blaring. And the tourists had all gone home weeks before. Rumors of marauding pirates can have that effect on a little seaside town.

Worst of all, the police were still baffled. Chief Inspector Klewless had made a list of all the things he knew for certain — it wasn't very long.

Raid on archaeological dig—
    May 14
Raid on museum—June 12
Both raids happened under a
    full moon
Nothing seen on camera
Next full moon—TOMORROW!

Since the robbery, the residents of Dull-on-Sea had been making sure everything they owned was under lock and key. The bank had no space left in its vault, and every safety-deposit box was full.

On the way home from school, Matilda and her mom walked past the bank, where a line of people clutched their valuables. The line stretched around the corner, down the hill, around another corner, and along the seafront.

Everyone in the line looked nervously out to sea and muttered unintelligible nonsense about pirates. Mrs. Penelope Wise, the bank manager, was trying to persuade people to go home since the bank had no more room.

"It's a good thing we don't have anything valuable in our house," said Matilda's mom as they climbed on the bus. The bus was jam-packed, but they squished themselves between people on their way to the hardware store to stock up on padlocks.

The traffic was crawling along. Hundreds of cars wound around the traffic circle and spewed out along the main road, blocking the bus lane. People beeped their horns and shouted out of car windows, desperate to get to Do-It-All World.

At the Do-It-All World bus stop, a man from the store got on the bus.

"I'm sorry to tell you that we've completely sold out of padlocks . . . and window locks . . . and door chains . . . and door bolts . . . and hammers . . . and nails. . . . Oh, and mini-safes."

A crowd of people waiting to get off the bus let out a loud moan before ambling back to their seats. A few more people climbed aboard, laden with bags, and stood in the aisle looking smug.

"I couldn't get a mini-safe, so I'm going to glue my doors shut!" said a lady beside Matilda, clutching two plastic bags full of superglue. "Those pirates will never get in if I glue the doors shut!"

"What if they come down the chimney?" said her friend, a bag of cement at her feet and several hefty iron chains slung over her shoulder. "And how will YOU get OUT of the house if they do?"

Matilda and her mom got off the bus at the end of their street. Mr. Shaw, at number 34, was up a ladder, fitting cameras under his eaves. He'd already boarded up his windows.

"Better safe than sorry," he shouted down. "I've met nice pirates in my time, but generally, they're a bunch of rogues!"

As they walked to their front door, Matilda noticed Miss Pinky, who lived across the street, struggling out of her garage with a large box. Miss Pinky was nearly one hundred

years old, and the box looked far too heavy
for a lady of her years.

"Shall we go and help her?" Matilda
asked her mom.

"That would be a very
kind thing to do, Tilda,"
said Mom.

1.
MISS PINKY

"Hello! Would you like some help with that box?" Matilda asked as she skipped up Miss Pinky's driveway.

"Oh, thank you, dear," said Miss Pinky as Matilda supported one edge of the box. "I don't want those pesky pirates to take any of Stanley's war medals."

"Is there anything else you'd like some help with?" asked Matilda's mom.

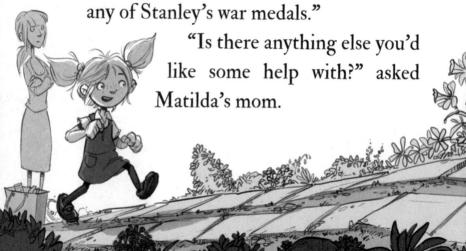

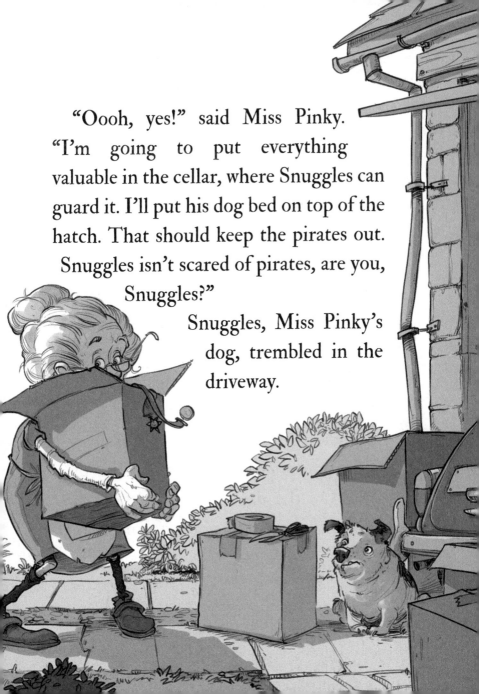

"Oooh, yes!" said Miss Pinky. "I'm going to put everything valuable in the cellar, where Snuggles can guard it. I'll put his dog bed on top of the hatch. That should keep the pirates out. Snuggles isn't scared of pirates, are you, Snuggles?"

Snuggles, Miss Pinky's dog, trembled in the driveway.

Matilda and her mom spent the next hour carrying things down into Miss Pinky's cellar. Miss Pinky's house was the only house on the street that actually had a cellar. Miss Pinky and her brother, Stanley, had refused to sell their home when the land was being developed, so the builders had just built all the new houses around them. Miss Pinky's house was full to the brim with old things, tucked in every nook and cranny.

Under the bed was a suitcase crammed with more money than Matilda had ever seen. On the dresser was a jewelry box overflowing with gold chains, rings, and bracelets that were encrusted with sapphires and rubies. In a tray on the kitchen window ledge was a beautiful silver watch on a chain, strung with small medallions. Paintings in ornate frames hung on the walls. A pineapple-shaped cookie jar on the sideboard held a diamond-encrusted tiara that Miss Pinky said had been a gift from a nice gentleman just before the Second World War. She said she still liked to wear it sometimes when she listened to her gramophone.

Once everything was packed away in the cellar, Miss Pinky slammed the hatch shut and secured it with a huge padlock. Matilda then helped her pull the carpet over the trapdoor, and they placed Snuggles's bed and bowl on top of the carpet. But Snuggles was nowhere to be seen.

"I'm sure he'll appear soon," said Miss Pinky. "Now, who'd like a nice cup of tea? Perhaps a bottle of soda for young Matilda?"

"That would be lovely," said Matilda's mom.

"And a piece of cake?" asked Miss Pinky.

"Oh, no, thank you. We haven't had our dinner yet, and cake will ruin Tilda's appetite."

As Matilda gazed around the now-empty room, wishing she could have a piece of cake, Miss Pinky clattered around the kitchen. Then she emerged again, shuffling quickly across the dining room toward a large built-in cupboard.

"The kettle's on — it won't be a minute," she muttered. "Now, where's the key for that padlock? We don't want any pesky pirates finding it, not after all that trouble we've been to."

She opened the cupboard door and Matilda saw a huge jumble of keys dangling from several rows of hooks. Miss Pinky rummaged through them and plucked out a large key on a chain, which she hung around her neck.

But another key instantly caught Matilda's eye. It was enormous and rusty, with a skull carved into its head. She was just about to ask what it was for when the kettle started whistling and Miss Pinky closed the cupboard door and trotted off to make tea.

Back home and tucked up in bed, Matilda couldn't stop thinking about pirates. She wondered if Jim had received her letter. When would he get here? She turned off her light and tried to get comfy. She lay on her back. She lay on her side. She shuffled her pillows, pulled her blanket up over her chin, and closed her eyes really, really tight.

Just as Matilda was thinking that she'd never get to sleep, there was a loud "Squawk!" outside her window.

"You made me jump!" said Matilda to the parrot perched on her window ledge. She picked up the roll of parchment that had fallen from his beak, broke the wax seal, and unfurled a note from Jim Lad.

5.
THE BLACKHOLE

It was nine o'clock on Saturday morning, and Matilda was waiting at the end of the harbor wall, clutching a satchel stuffed with newspaper clippings. She had caught a bus to town with her dad, who had popped into the hardware store to see if they had more padlocks in stock — just in case the pirates had any interest in lawn mowers.

Matilda saw the sails of the *Blackhole* appear on the horizon, and her heart skipped a beat. Jim Lad would be in the crow's nest with Bones, his wooden-legged dog. She wondered if he could already see her through his telescope. She waved just in case.

"They were still sold out of padlocks," Dad groaned as he returned with a still-empty bag. "I'll have to use your bike lock to secure the shed, if we're going to keep my lawn mower safe from pirates. Talking of pirates, are those the Jolley-Rogers heading our way?"

He sat beside Matilda on a bench, and they watched together as the *Blackhole* neared. They could see tiny figures aloft, furling sails and being thrown from side to side as the hull rolled in the surf.

Even with the ship in view, it seemed like an eternity to Matilda before the *Blackhole* eventually arrived in Dull-on-Sea, waves breaking across her bow as she turned in to the harbor. All the sails were furled and Matilda could hear the slow, rhythmic chug of the engine. Jim's little sister, Nugget, was at the wheel, standing on a barrel of grog.

"AHOY!" yelled Jim Lad, who was balancing on a yard, steadying himself by holding on to a rope.

Matilda jumped up from the bench and ran along the harbor wall, keeping pace with the ship. Bones was barking excitedly from the crow's nest. Jim grabbed another rope and slid from a great height down onto the bowsprit.

"MATILDA!" he shouted with a broad, gap-toothed grin.

He scuttled toward the deck and ducked beneath the rail. When he reappeared, he was holding a coil of rope across one arm, and in his other hand he had a knotted ball, which formed the end of the rope.

"CATCH, TILLY!"

The knotted ball bounced along the cobbles, and Matilda grabbed hold of it and pulled more rope toward her. She wrapped it around a mooring and held tight, nervously waiting for the *Blackhole* to pick up the slack.

At the stern, Jim's dad jumped ashore with another coil, shouting directions to Nugget, who was belting out a sea chantey as she steered the ship against the harbor wall. Jim and his mom scurried around on deck, pulling the other ends of the ropes, and in no time at all the *Blackhole* was safely moored.

Jim didn't have the patience to wait for his dad to unhitch the gangplank, so he grabbed a loose rope and swung across to Matilda, landing right in front of her on the quay.

"I read everyone yer note, Tilly," he said, breathless. "My grandpa thinks he knows the scoundrels. Come aboard and he'll tell ye all about it. My dad'll drive you home afterward."

"Would that be right with yerself, mister?" Jim said to Matilda's dad, who mumbled a quiet "Um . . . OK. . . ." as Jim grabbed Matilda's bag and pulled her up the gangplank.

6.
GRANDPA'S TALE

Matilda had met Grandpa Rogers before, but he was older and more gnarly than she remembered. The dim candlelight cast shadows across his face, which cracked into a toothless grin at the sight of her.

"ARRR . . . Matilda," Grandpa said. "I hear ye've got a pirate problem?"

"*I* don't have a pirate problem, Mr. Rogers," said Matilda. "But Dull-on-Sea does have one."

Matilda pulled the newspaper clippings from her satchel. Eyewitness Mervyn Wobley had helped the police put together a sketch of the pirate captain, which had been on the front page of all the papers a month before.

Grandpa scratched his chin with his hook as he squinted at the clipping.

"ARRR, just as I suspected. . . . If it ain't Ol' Twirly!"

"Ol' Twirly?" asked Jim.

"Aye, but he'd be Cap'n Twirlybeard to you, boy," Grandpa said, "or he'd be cuttin' out yer tongue and feedin' it to the fishes!

"Y'see, Jim Lad, in the good old days, Cap'n Twirlybeard and his crew were the scourge of the seas. Their ship, the *Black Rat*, was lightning fast and brimmin' with cannons. All feared Ol' Twirly's flag, and many thought him invincible." Grandpa waved his hook in the air.

"But one fateful day, he and his crew were ambushed ashore by His Majesty's Marines. 'Tis said they fought to the last, and Ol' Twirly his'self was the last pirate standing. But even with his crew slain around him, he refused to surrender. . . ." Grandpa smiled. "Y'know, I thinks I can remember a chantey that tells the tale. Would ye like to hear it?"

Matilda and Jim nodded excitedly. "Sing it, Grandpa!"

Grandpa Rogers plucked a battered concertina from beside his chair. He cleared his throat with a hollow cough, and after gargling some grog, he began.

"They say Ol' Twirly's fought his last,
Paid the price for his piratin' past.
The king's men took him on dry land,
Ambushed for a final stand.

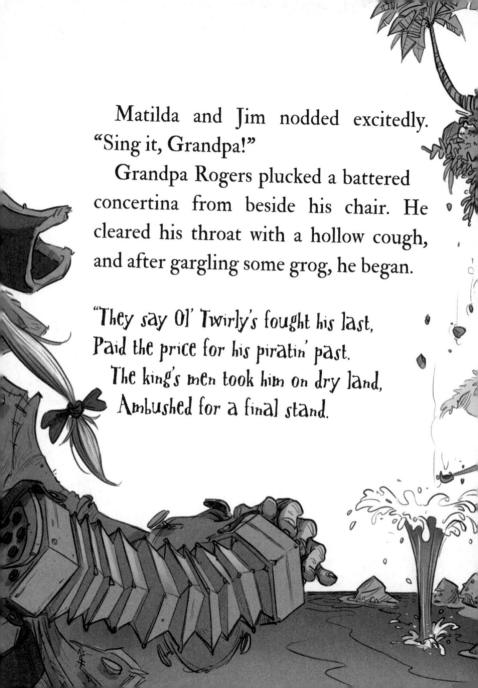

Outnumbered twenty men to one,
Soon his crew were dead and gone.
Ol' Twirly clung to a clifftop tree,
Blade in hand, his back to the sea.

Muskets filled the air with sound,
Blew Ol' Twirly off the ground,
Down and down from the cliff he fell,
To his death, cursed to hell. . . .

No sign of Twirly was found below,
Though they searched both high and low.
They found a key, they found his hat.
They sank the *Black Rat* where it sat.

'Neath the waves, they found his gold,
But the seabed had too strong a hold.
The chest was stuck in a seaweed cave,
So they left it in its watery grave.

The navy ship was England bound
When it sank with the key in Dullshire Sound —
Smashed to bits against the shore,
Swallowed by sands forevermore.

They say Ol' Twirly searches still
And his ghostly crew won't rest until
They find the key they lost that day
That will save their souls — so they say...."

Grandpa coughed a little, laid down his concertina, and took a swig of grog.

"So it all comes down to a key?" asked Jim Lad.

"Aye," said Grandpa. "A key with a carved skull for its head: the Key of Souls! It unlocks the giant treasure chest that sat in the hold of the *Black Rat*. Legend has it that only by opening that chest, the Chest of Souls, can Ol' Twirly be released from his ghostly life. So he'll be wantin' his key back."

"But ain't Captain Twirlybeard long dead?" said Jim.

"ARRR, he be lonnnng dead, Jim Lad, but he and his crew ain't had no rest," said Grandpa. "They ain't normal pirates like you and I, Jim. . . . They be GHOST PIRATES! They appear at every full moon for just one night, then they vanish till the next full moon comes round."

Jim's jaw dropped, but Matilda was deep in thought. "A carved skull?" she whispered.

"Aye, what of it, girl?" Grandpa turned to Matilda.

I've seen the key. I know where it is!

7.
A Plan

Jim Lad and Matilda were in the captain's cabin, beneath the poop deck. The captain's table was strewn with paper, pens, maps, and empty potato chip bags. It had taken all afternoon, twelve cookies (each), a large bottle of cream soda, two apples, four bananas, and plenty of chips to come up with a plan.

Jim unfolded his map of Dull-on-Sea.

"So, where be Miss Pinky's house?" he asked, pencil in one hand, compass in the other. "And she keeps the Key of Souls in her cupboard, y'say?"

"Yeah," answered Matilda. "Like I said, it was just hanging there. I don't think she has any idea."

She pointed to her street on the map.

"Right, methinks we need to pay Miss Pinky a visit," said Jim.

Jim and Matilda walked out on deck and saw a police officer shuffling uneasily up the gangplank.

"Dad!" Jim Lad called out.

His dad's grimy face popped up from a hatch in the middle of the deck. "Blinkin' engines!" he grumbled.

"Good afternoon, Mr. Jolley-Rogers," said the officer.

"ARRR, g'day to ye!" said Jim's dad.

"We've had a few robberies in Dull-on-Sea of late, and it would appear that the perpetrators were of a piratey persuasion," said

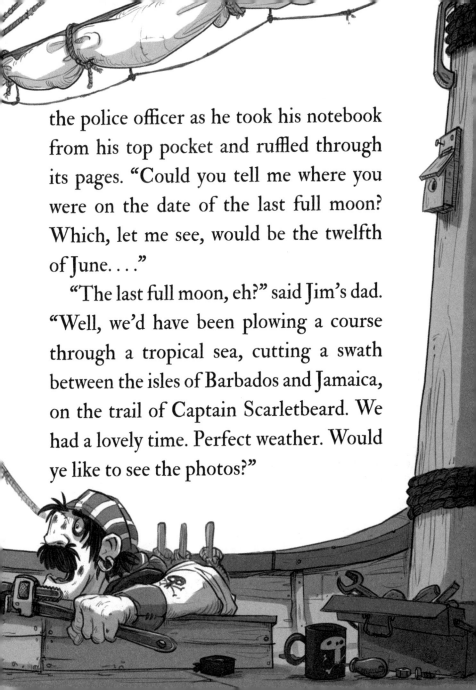

the police officer as he took his notebook from his top pocket and ruffled through its pages. "Could you tell me where you were on the date of the last full moon? Which, let me see, would be the twelfth of June. . . ."

"The last full moon, eh?" said Jim's dad. "Well, we'd have been plowing a course through a tropical sea, cutting a swath between the isles of Barbados and Jamaica, on the trail of Captain Scarletbeard. We had a lovely time. Perfect weather. Would ye like to see the photos?"

"Um, I see. . . ." said the officer. "And did anyone see you on your adventure?"

"Well, there'd be that scurviest of sea dogs, Scarletbeard himself. I'm sure the hen-hearted varmint would give me an alibi, if that's the cut of yer jib. Would ye like his e-mail address? Or I think my wife may have his cell number."

Jim's dad cupped his mouth with both hands as he bellowed aloft, "DARLIN'! DO YE HAVE SCARLETBEARD'S NUMBER?"

"OH, YES, I'M SURE I DO. ALTHOUGH AFTER THAT BUSINESS IN BARBADOS, I DON'T THINK HE'LL WANT TO CHAT" came a distant reply. "IF YOU GIVE ME TEN MINUTES TO FINISH THIS

SPLICING, I CAN LOOK IT UP ON MY PHONE. . . ."

"Well, um . . . I'll just pop back, but here's my card," said the police constable. "Oh, and one more thing, the folks in Dull-on-Sea are a little nervous about pirates right now. You might be better mooring in the bay rather than on the quayside. We don't want any incidents."

And with that, he stuffed his notebook into his top pocket and strolled off to town.

"Dad," Jim said, "Tilly and I have a plan, but we need to go see Miss Pinky first. And can Tilly come for a sleepover tonight? We need her to be here for our plan to work."

"Aye, of course she can, lad!" said Jim's dad. "Right, then, time is short if we be needin' to move the *Blackhole* out the harbor. Let's get ashore, and ye can tell me yer plan on the way to Matilda's house."

Climbing down lots of ladders, they made their way into the belly of the ship. Jim Lad pushed open a heavy door to reveal a room full of barrels, chests, and cannons. In the middle of it all stood the Jolley-Rogers' amphibious vehicle.

Jim hopped into the back and shouted, "Climb aboard, Tilly!"

Nugget pulled a lever on the wall, then leaped into the vehicle and strapped

herself into her seat. The stern of the ship slowly opened up.

"Hold tight, me hearties!" bellowed Jim's dad as the vehicle surged out of the ship and splashed into the murky water.

In no time, they had crossed the harbor and were trundling through Dull-on-Sea, leaving a trail of water, barnacles, and seaweed behind them.

Before long, Jim's dad was pulling tight the handbrake outside Matilda's house. Jim Lad and Matilda jumped out and crossed the road to Miss Pinky's.

Jim's dad lifted Nugget out of the vehicle and flip-flopped to Matilda's front door. He rang the doorbell and told Nugget to be on her best behavior.

Matilda's dad opened the door, wearing an apron and a pair of dish-washing gloves.

Nugget poked Matilda's dad in the tummy with her wooden sword. "Does that protect landlubbers from pirates?" she asked, staring at his apron.

"The urchins are off to parley with Miss Pinky, but if it's OK with you, Matilda is welcome t'sleep over on the *Blackhole*," said Jim's dad, eyeing Matilda's dad suspiciously. "Tonight, perhaps? Bein' a scurvy Saturday, and a full moon 'n' all?"

"Um, well . . . I . . . er . . . I suppose that would be fine," said Matilda's dad. "I should probably check with her mom, but she's at her yoga class, so I won't bother her. Shall we pick Matilda up in the morning?"

"Don't worry yerself," said Jim's dad. "We can bring 'er back on the morrow."

"Um, would you like to come inside

while I pack Matilda an overnight bag?" said her dad.

"We'll wait here," explained Jim's dad. "Young Nugget don't like yer brick-built homes, and she has a tendency toward destruction. She'll be happier in the open air, I'd say."

8.
THE KEY OF SOULS

Jim decided that Miss Pinky's front room was hotter than cooking belowdecks in the tropics. Two bars on her electric fire glowed bright orange, and he wondered why she needed it on at all in the middle of July.

"Ooh, it's a bit nippy out there, isn't it?" said Miss Pinky. "Would you like some lemon cake, dears? It's just finished baking."

Jim looked at Matilda. Matilda looked at Jim.

"Yes, please!" they chirped in unison.

"And what would you like with it? Cup of tea? Or soda?"

"Soda, please!" said Matilda.

"Grog, if ye please!" said Jim with a cheeky grin.

"Soda and grog. . . . Hmm," said Miss Pinky as she shuffled off to the kitchen.

After much crashing, gurgling, jingling, and jangling, Miss Pinky reappeared pushing a small cart, on which sat a moist and sticky-looking lemon cake, three plates with three forks, a teapot, one cup, one saucer, a small milk jug, a sugar bowl with a silver teaspoon, two large pitchers, two glasses, and a heavily decorated cookie tin.

"I haven't got any grog, dear. I've got

soda or homemade lemonade. Or a nice cup of tea. I've got some cookies too. Do you like cookies? I've had them a little while. My brother Stanley liked cookies, but he died in 1981. These were his favorites, and there are still a few left!"

Jim and Matilda decided to stick to the cake.

"So, Matilda dear, what can I do for you?" Miss Pinky inquired.

"Miss Pinky," began Matilda, "we'd like to borrow one of your keys."

"One of my keys?" said Miss Pinky, opening the key-cupboard door and looking puzzled. "Which one?"

Before Miss Pinky could say anything else, Jim shouted, "It's the Key of Souls! The big one, with the skull — that's the Key of Souls!"

"Souls, you say? Well, I never, so that's what it's for. . . ." mumbled Miss Pinky. "What do you mean by 'souls,' Jim dear?"

"It unlocks the Chest of Souls, and when the key is turned, it will send those ghosts to Davy Jones's locker!"

"The Chest of Souls, eh? Ghosts, you say? Davy Jones's locker? How peculiar. You young people say some funny things. . . . My brother found this key on the beach, near Parrot Point, I think.

"He loved this key, did Stanley. We used to have it on the mantelpiece, but the skull gave me the heebie-jeebies, so I moved it to the cupboard when Stanley passed away."

Miss Pinky took the Key of Souls from its hook and examined it carefully. "He found it taking part in military exercises during the war. The spring of 1944. I remember him saying how they were practicing beach landings for D-day and using live ammunition. Terribly dangerous, it was. Stanley told me that he and his pal Joe were lying on the beach, trying to get the sand out of their rifles. They were shaking like Jell-O with all those bullets flying around when a shell landed twenty feet away. Gave them the fright of their lives, it did. And among all the sand and stones in the explosion, this almighty key flew through the air and

bounced off Stanley's helmet with a clonk. Lucky he had it on, he said. The key put a big dent in it; could just as well have been his head. Fancy that. . . . The Key of Souls."

"Can we borrow it?" asked Matilda.

"It's those pirates, you see," added Jim Lad. "Those scurvy dogs that raided the museum. We think this is what they be after. They'll keep on coming too. They won't rest until they find the key, miss!"

"Well, I suppose it is normally just tucked away in the cupboard. Although it does remind me of dear old Stanley," said Miss Pinky. "But maybe I wouldn't miss it for a little while. . . ."

Miss Pinky handed the Key of Souls to Matilda.

"Thank you! By the way, have you found Snuggles?" asked Matilda.

"Not a peep," said Miss Pinky with a sigh.

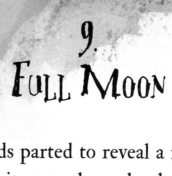

9.
FULL MOON

The clouds parted to reveal a full moon. A bowsprit cut through the swirling fog, dragging a tattered sail beneath it. A hulking ship followed closely behind, crashing in the waves and creaking as if it were begging the sea to break it apart.

Shadowy figures busied themselves aloft, while others took arms from the quartermaster on deck: flintlocks, pikes, muskets, and cutlasses.

Then came an urgent call from the crow's nest: "SHIP AHOY, CAP'N!"

A gigantic figure hanging from the rigging, blade in hand and shrouded in mist, bellowed, "HARD TO PORT!"

Almost at once, the *Black Rat* turned sharply in a shower of spray and brine, firing tendrils of fog across the water toward the *Blackhole*, which had been positioned directly in the path of Twirlybeard's ship.

On the deck of the *Blackhole,* the Jolley-Rogers watched nervously. Apart from Nugget, who wasn't nervous at all and couldn't wait to meet a real-life ghost.

"FLY!" ordered Grandpa, and he launched his trusty parrot, Squawk, toward the *Black Rat,* a rolled-up parchment in his talons.

"Do you think they'll come?" Jim Lad's mom asked Grandpa.

"When Cap'n Twirlybeard reads that note, he'll come, all right," Grandpa replied.

The Jolley-Rogers waited in the moonlight. All was silent but for the waves lapping against the oak of the *Blackhole*'s hull and the gentle creak of its timbers.

After a few minutes, Nugget shouted, "Squawk!" and pointed toward the *Black Rat*'s stern, where a parrot's silhouette could be seen heading their way.

Squawk landed on Grandpa's hand. "Squawk!" he screeched. "Coming aboarrrrd! Avast and belay! Ol' Twirly wants a key today!"

The Jolley-Rogers watched as, across the water, figures tumbled into boats, waving cutlasses and flintlocks, their briny grumblings drifting on the mist.

A voice boomed, "Heave ho!" and Captain Twirlybeard and his crew lurched toward the *Blackhole*.

On the leeward side of the *Blackhole,* Jim
and Matilda scurried down a rope ladder
and into a rowboat, where Bones waited
for them, his tail wagging furiously.

"Shhhh!" said Jim before Bones had a
chance to bark.

Matilda was both excited
and terrified. She wasn't

usually out after dark; her mom and dad were probably fast asleep already.

"Soon as they reach t'other side of the *Blackhole,* we'll be off," said Jim as he readied the oars. "I'll row fast and wide, deep in the fog, so they don't see us under that moon. When we get to the *Black Rat,* I'll throw up the grappling hook and we'll climb aboard. Got it?"

Matilda nodded. She didn't know if she had enough strength to climb a rope, but she couldn't wait to try.

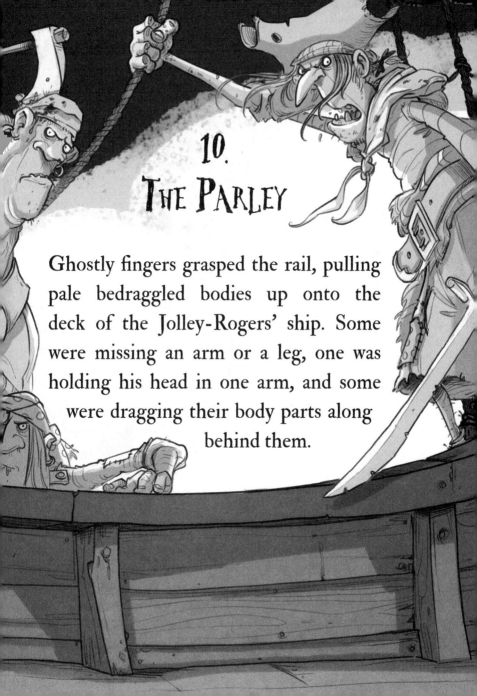

10.
THE PARLEY

Ghostly fingers grasped the rail, pulling pale bedraggled bodies up onto the deck of the Jolley-Rogers' ship. Some were missing an arm or a leg, one was holding his head in one arm, and some were dragging their body parts along behind them.

Dead eyes stared at the Jolley-Rogers from beneath lank, dripping locks of hair.

"Coooool!" said Nugget.

Jim's dad gasped, drawing Jim's mom near.

"I'm scared...." he said.

"We'll be fine," said Jim's mom. "I'm sure Grandpa knows what he's doing."

Grandpa stood firm on the deck, arms folded, Squawk clinging to his shoulder.

"SO!" bellowed the ghost captain, who had the most enormous curly beard. "You called us for a parley! SPEAK, old man! While I still have the mind to listen."

Grandpa gripped the key in his pocket. "They say that you've been searchin' for a key, Cap'n Twirlybeard."

"Aye. That may be so," said Captain Twirlybeard. "What of it?"

"I'd like to make ye a deal, Cap'n," Grandpa continued. "I can give ye the key, if ye leave the good folk of Dull-on-Sea be and return their treasures."

"ARRRRR!" roared the captain, the coils of his curly beard swaying like snakes. "Ye can curse me for a lubber, but that there implies that ye'll be knowing the where'bouts of MY key. . . . WHERE BE IT? Y'should remember, old man, I ain't renowned for my patience."

Grandpa didn't back down. "I'll give ye the key if you return the treasures of Dull-on-Sea and leave these shores. Do we have a deal?" he asked, pulling the

Key of Souls from his pocket and holding it up in the air.

Twirlybeard's one good eye lit up at the sight of the key. "Ye see, old man, we've become rather partial to our life of ghostly piratin'. We don't want no rest! We can raid and pillage, whilst no soul can hurt us. I'll still be takin' my scurvy crew ashore tonight. There's plenty of plunder left in the town of Dull-on-Sea." Twirlybeard's good eye glinted with evil. "And I'll be taking my key anyhows; I don't want another to possess it. When it be hung around my neck, no one can use it to unlock the Chest of Souls, and me 'n' my scurvy crew can go piratin' for all

eternity! We'll NEVER be sent to Davy
Jones's locker!"

"I take it that's a no to a deal, then,"
said Grandpa with a sigh.

"GIVE ME THE KEY OR I'LL SPLIT YE STARBOARD TO LARBOARD! YE'LL FEEL MY BLADE, YE BILGE RAT!"

Twirlybeard rose up a full seven feet tall, puffing out his chest and blowing cold air from his nostrils. All around him, dead hands drew cutlasses from scabbards, pulled daggers from belts, and pointed flintlocks in Grandpa's direction.

"SQUAWK!" said Squawk.

Grandpa stood firm.

Jim's dad fainted.

11.
ABOARD THE GHOSTLY GALLEON

Jim Lad steered the rowboat against
the far side of the *Black Rat*, cautiously
pulling up against her timbers
as she bobbed and creaked
and tugged at her anchor.

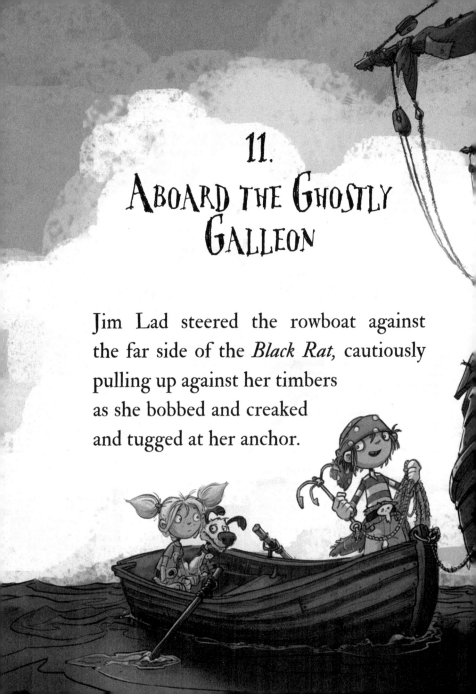

The ship was solid, but Jim noticed it had a strange shimmer around it. He reached out and touched the hull. It felt real enough.

"Stand back, Tilly," he warned as he took the grappling hook from his leather bag. In one smooth motion, he hurled the hook upward through the fog. There was a wood-splitting clunk as it caught hold of the *Black Rat*'s rail.

"I'll go first, Tilly, then you follow me up. Bones, you stay 'ere and guard the boat. If ye hear anythin' or see any of them ghosts, you bark good and loud."

"Yip!" barked Bones quietly.

Matilda tried to look confident, but her hands were trembling. As Jim shuffled up the knotted rope, she grabbed hold of it behind him.

Pretty quickly, Matilda decided that she didn't like climbing ropes. Her arms were on fire and the coarse rope hurt her hands. On top of that, the ship was covered in limpets, barnacles, and slimy seaweed, which were making a real mess of her tights.

Jim, already at the top, whispered encouragement over the rail.

Finally, with her palms as red as beets and seaweed sticking to her knees, she dragged herself over the rail and onto the deck.

Jim was hitching up a block and tackle. "To lower the booty into our boat," he said.

But they had to find the booty first....

Matilda gazed into the eerie stillness. In the moonlight, the rigging cast long, dark shadows across the deck. Masts and yards towered above them, hastily furled sails flapped in the breeze, just visible through the fog, while ropes and chains clattered against one another.

"Where do we start?" she whispered.

"We'll try the cargo hold first," Jim replied.

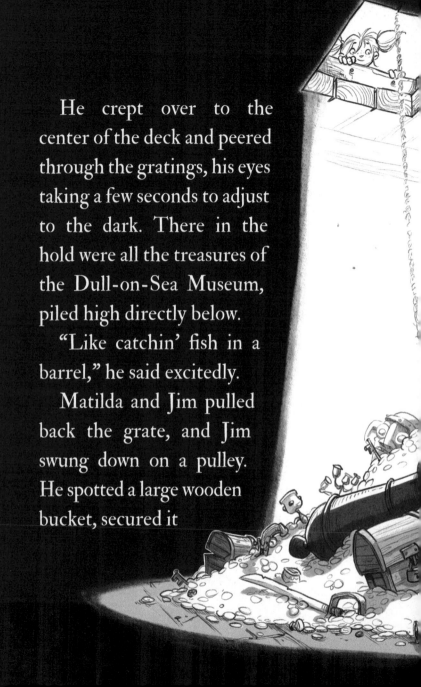

He crept over to the center of the deck and peered through the gratings, his eyes taking a few seconds to adjust to the dark. There in the hold were all the treasures of the Dull-on-Sea Museum, piled high directly below.

"Like catchin' fish in a barrel," he said excitedly.

Matilda and Jim pulled back the grate, and Jim swung down on a pulley. He spotted a large wooden bucket, secured it to the pulley, and then started loading it with booty. "Hoist away, Tilly!"

Matilda found it surprisingly easy to raise the bucket, even with the weight of all the treasure. Once she had emptied it out she lowered the rope for Jim to fill up again. And again. And again. And again . . .

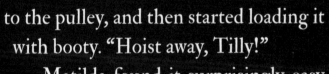

Before long, Jim and Matilda were both on deck, admiring their handiwork — a great pile of treasure that would shortly be returned to the museum.

Matilda climbed back down into the rowboat, and Jim started lowering the treasure to her.

"Who'd have thought it'd be so easy?" exclaimed Jim. "Those powder-brained squabs are still natterin' 'bout their key while we're lootin' their hold!"

"It's odd that they didn't leave a lookout," commented Matilda.

"Nah," replied Jim. "They wouldn't expect no raid on a ghost ship. We caught 'em nappin'! Just one final load and we'll be —"

CLANG, CLANG, CLANG!

CLANG, CLANG, CLANG!

The *Black Rat*'s bell rang loud from the quarterdeck, echoing through the night air.

Jim and Matilda were not alone.

Back on board the *Blackhole,* the Jolley-Rogers were surrounded. Countless blades and blackened muzzles were inches from Grandpa's nose.

But then, across the waves, came the harsh sound of the *Black Rat*'s bell.

Twirlybeard's crew turned in the direction of their ship, dropping their weapons a little. In that split second, Grandpa passed the Key of Souls to Squawk, who took flight for the ghost ship.

"TREACHERY!" Captain Twirlybeard boomed, swinging his cutlass in vain at the passing parrot. "Lock these swivel-tongued scugs belowdecks and let's get back to the *Rat,* boys!"

Pressing his grisly face against Grandpa's, Twirlybeard growled, "An' I'll be back for ye 'n' all! When I've cleared the *Rat* of varmin' and got me'self MY key, I'll be back for ye and yer gizzards!"

12.
THE DUEL

On the *Black Rat*, Jim was about to make his escape when a blur of colored feathers zipped by, dropping something onto the floor in front of him. The Key of Souls!

As Jim stuffed the key into his belt, a gunshot whizzed past his head and cut a rope clean in two.

"Hold it right there, laddie!" a voice creaked. "Ye

woke me from me slumber, and ye seems to be takin' things tha' don't belong to ye."

He turned to see a hunched, peg-legged figure, waving a flintlock in his direction. Jim took a deep breath and grabbed a cutlass from a nearby bucket. He'd never had a real duel before, but he'd practiced with his dad, who said he had lots of potential. He hoped that it would be enough. . . .

"Fight me fair, ye curmudgeon! I'm a boy and ye seem to be a man," taunted Jim as he jumped down from the rail.

The old pirate chuckled and stuck his flintlock in his belt. He took a swig of grog and drew his sword.

The two opponents eyed each other across the deck, gripping their weapons tightly and inching closer.

Now that he was a bit nearer, Jim didn't like the look of the old pirate at all. He had a scar that ran across his face, and one ear was hanging off. He was panting heavily, drool oozing from his mouth.

Jim Lad felt beads of sweat running down his forehead. But before their cutlasses could clash, a great, booming voice echoed through the fog at the far end of the deck.

"YOU'LL LEAVE HIM FER ME!" ordered Captain Twirlybeard, striding toward them, a cutlass in each hand. His motley crew of ghost pirates followed behind him.

If Jim was sweating at the thought of fighting the peg-legged pirate, he was terrified at the prospect of taking on Twirlybeard. Whatever potential his dad thought he might have, it probably wasn't enough to take on one of the most fearsome pirates who had ever lived.

But before Jim could think about it properly, two cutlasses came flying toward him. It took all his strength to parry them. He lost his footing and fell to the deck, then scurried behind the mast as one of Twirlybeard's blades cut a great chunk from the timber. Jim took a swing at his foe, but Twirlybeard effortlessly brushed it aside. "That all ye got, boy?" He grinned. "This won't take long!"

Jim Lad leaped for the rigging and climbed up with one hand while parrying blows with the cutlass in the other.

"GET DOWN HERE AND FIGHT, YE VARMINT!" yelled Twirlybeard. "OR I'LL BE COMING TO GET YE!"

Throwing down one of his cutlasses, he began to climb after Jim. The rigging groaned under his mighty bulk.

In the rowboat below, Matilda and Bones listened to the clash of cutlasses, unable to see who was winning. Suddenly, Bones flew from Matilda's arms and up the side of the ship, claws scratching against the barnacles. He squeezed beneath the rail and ran straight at the ghostly crew, barking furiously. "Woof! Woof! Woof!"

High up in the rigging, Jim could hear Bones.

"Yer mutt can't save you now, boy," the captain warned. "Gimme that key and I'll leave yer heart still beatin' in yer puny body. But if you don't, I'll—"

Jim whistled and Bones looked up, wagging his tail as he ran around the deck, chased by the *Black Rat*'s scurvy crew. Jim glanced back at Captain Twirlybeard, who was only a cutlass's length away.

"You want the key, Cap'n? Then you'll have to be quick. . . . FETCH, Bones!" Jim yelled as he threw the key toward the deck. With some graceful doggy acrobatics, Bones caught it in midair, dodging several pairs of ghostly hands, a cutlass, and a rusty pike. And in almost the same movement, he disappeared below-decks, through an open hatch beneath the fo'c'sle.

A huge hand grabbed Jim around the neck. His legs swung fifty feet above the deck, and Captain Twirlybeard breathed a cold mist about his head.

"I should drop ye now!" Twirlybeard growled. "Yer whole scurvy family are scoundrels and skulks! Now, ye'll be getting that dog of yers back, and my key, or BLOW MY SCUTTLEBUTT, I'll feed ye to the sharks!"

Throwing Jim over his shoulder, Captain Twirlybeard slid down to the deck.

"Someone grab a hold of him, nice 'n' tight, and the rest of ye — search the ship!" he ordered. "And check overboard! Our booty's still 'ere somewhere, and that flea-bitten dog can't get far!"

13.
Jim, the Captive

From the rowboat, Matilda could hear feet shuffling across the deck above, heading toward where the grappling hook and rope hung from the *Black Rat*'s rail.

Her heart beat hard against her ribs. Could she row fast enough to escape? She'd never rowed a boat before — the ghostly pirates would definitely catch her.

She thought about swimming for it instead. She'd recently got her fifty-yard badge at swim club, but it was probably more than fifty yards back to the *Blackhole*.

Then she thought of Jim. She couldn't leave him.

Looking above her head, she spotted a row of closed gun ports, secured by lengths of twine. She grabbed a rusty cutlass, cut through the twine of the nearest port, and pushed it open above

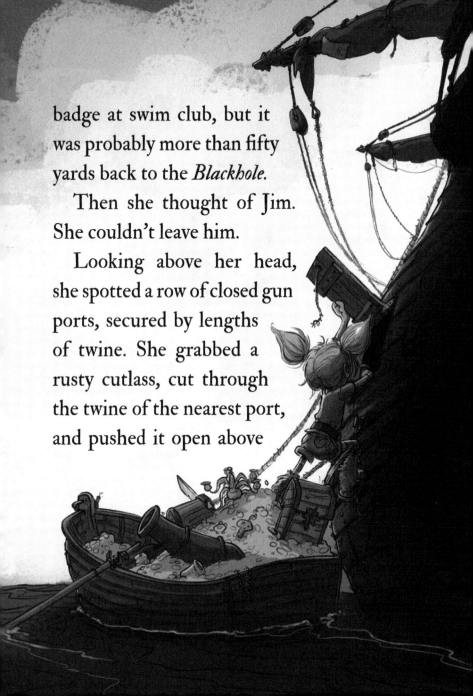

her head. She jumped up and pulled her head and shoulders through the hole, grabbing the nearest cannon with one hand.

It was cold and damp and inky black inside. The *Black Rat*'s gun deck was the last place Matilda wanted to be, but she had to help Jim, so she dragged the rest of her body through the gun port.

She was just in time.

"There's a rowboat down 'ere, Cap'n! Loaded high with our booty!" a scurvy pirate shouted from up on deck.

"Shall we bring it back aboard?"

"JUST FIND ME THAT DOG! I WANT MY KEY!" ordered Captain Twirlybeard. "The treasure can wait."

Matilda heard scratching but it was so dark that she couldn't see what it was. She hoped it wasn't rats. Pirate ships were always full of rats.

Then she heard something scuttling toward her.

She froze.

It licked her face.

"Woof!" said Bones as he dropped something at Matilda's feet.

Back on deck, Jim was relieved that Matilda hadn't been found in the rowboat. But where was she? He doubted she would try to swim. The water was cold, and it was a long way back to the *Blackhole*. She must have gotten on board somehow.

Jim's thoughts were interrupted by Captain Twirlybeard, twirling his beard menacingly in his fingers.

"As for ye, boy, we've got all the time in the world. We need that key, but if yer still on board at sunrise, ye'll be joinin' us for a long, long month of darkness. That'll give us plenty of time to find yer mutt and the key. And maybe . . . if luck deserts ye . . . ye'll be joining us for a lot longer than that! ARRRRR!"

The surrounding crew guffawed. Jim wondered what Captain Twirlybeard meant. Would he be stuck aboard the *Black Rat*, with its deadly crew, until the next full moon?

"ARRR, lads! Let's go on a DOG HUNT!" shouted Captain Twirlybeard, cutlass held high.

14.
THE CHEST OF SOULS

In the darkness, Matilda's hands closed around the object Bones had dropped. It was the key! But the thuds and shouts of the pirate crew were getting ever louder and closer.

Suddenly, Matilda could see candlelight bouncing against the joists and feet tumbling down some steps.

"Quick, Bones, we'd better hide!" she whispered, but Bones had already disappeared. Matilda was on her own.

And then it was too late. A huddle of ghostly pirates wielding cutlasses, muskets, and lanterns had spotted her and were advancing.

"We've found that key, Cap'n!" shouted a scrawny pirate who was missing an arm. "But it looks like we've got a stowaway. Ye'd better come see!"

More ghost pirates swarmed into the gun deck, armed to the teeth and chattering excitedly. But as soon as they saw Matilda, they stopped in their tracks.

Then louder thuds sounded and the steps groaned under a heavy weight. The pirate crowd parted and Twirlybeard

appeared. He was followed by his first mate, who had a firm hold of Jim.

"Look, lads," Twirlybeard said with a laugh. "It appears that Jim's wee doggy has turned itself into a young lady. . . ."

The pirates giggled, twitching nervously and gripping their weapons tight.

"But us piratin' types are a superstitious lot, and we don't like no girls on our ships. Shall we throw 'er overboard?"

The pirates roared their approval.

"TOSS 'ER IN THE SEA!"

"FEED 'ER TO THE SHARKS!"

"Give me that key, girl, and it'll save ye a drenchin'," said Twirlybeard as softly as he could.

Matilda held the key close and looked at Jim, struggling in the arms of the first mate. But he wasn't looking at her. He was looking beyond her, wide-eyed, to the far corner of the gun deck.

She turned to see what had caught his attention. There, glistening in the dim glow of the crew's lanterns, was a huge briny chest, entwined in ropes and chains and covered in barnacles. . . . The Chest of Souls!

"C'mon, girl, don't make me impatient! Give me that key!" roared Twirlybeard.

Matilda gripped the key even tighter. Twirlybeard was so close, his ghostly mist made her shiver. She stepped backward, almost tripping on a rope. She glanced again at the Chest of Souls.

"See now," grumbled Twirlybeard. "I'm startin' to wonder if a lubber like yerself knows what that key can do."

"Don't come too close. . . . Or . . . or . . . I'll . . ." mumbled Matilda nervously.

"Ye'll what?" Twirlybeard frowned. "Unlock the Chest of Souls? Take us down to the depths? End our miserable ghostly existence? Ye won't do nuthin'.

Gimme that key, little girl, or the boy will be sucked to Davy Jones's locker with us. . . . GIVE ME THE KEY!"

"He's lying, Tilly!" yelled Jim. "Open the —"

He was cut short by the first mate's hand across his mouth.

Matilda turned on her heels and ran, skipping over ropes and cannonballs. She had the key in her hand, and the Chest of Souls was so close. . . .

But Captain Twirlybeard was fast. He scooped Matilda up in his arms. She writhed, trying to escape his grip, but Twirlybeard had too firm a hold.

"Ye'll be goin' in the sea, lassie! And I'll

be taking that key," he said, snatching it from her hands. "Yer little pirate friend will be comin' with us to our ghostly grave. We need a new cabin boy, since we keelhauled the last one! ARRR, LADS! WE'VE GOT THE KEY!"

The crew cheered an almighty "OOO-ARRRR!" and waved their muskets and cutlasses in the air.

Twirlybeard held up the key triumphantly, with a wriggling Matilda tucked tightly under his other arm.

But even Captain Twirlybeard wasn't prepared for what came next.

"GRRRRR! WOOF!"

A bolt of black and white fur hurtled out of a nearby cannon, and Bones clamped his jaws onto Captain Twirlybeard's wooden leg. In his surprise, Twirlybeard dropped both Matilda and the key, shaking his leg frantically in an attempt to detach the very determined dog.

Matilda grabbed the key and pushed it into the lock on the chest. There was a satisfying click as she turned it.

Twirlybeard's good eye opened wide in terror as, with every scrap of her strength, Matilda heaved open the Chest of Souls.

The entire crew gasped and groaned. The first mate dropped Jim to the floor.

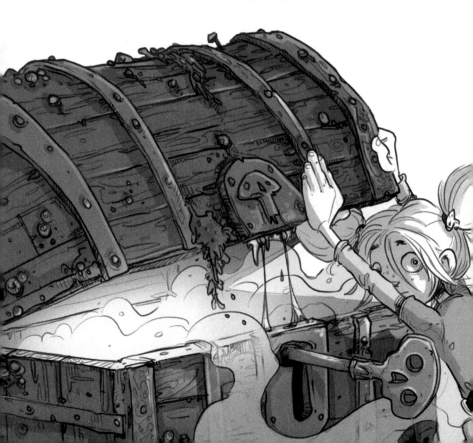

Almost immediately, seawater bubbled up through the deck. The pirates started to slide across the floor, tugged by a mysterious force toward the Chest of Souls.

Twirlybeard's fingernails scraped on a joist as he tried to cling to the timbers of his ship. Then he thrust his cutlass into the deck and gripped the hilt. But it was no good. His ghostly crew started tumbling into him as they were pulled toward the chest.

The water kept rising, casks and timber floating on its surface. Ropes and seaweed

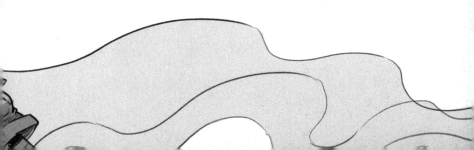

came to life and lashed around the pirates, encircling their arms and legs, yanking at any of them who were still resisting the tug of the chest.

"Quick, Jim!" shouted Matilda. "Follow Bones through the gun ports!"

As Jim splashed through the water toward Matilda, she glanced back to the seething mass of pirates, who were clinging to anything they could, including their captain, who was now enveloped in a bundle of tattered fabric, patches, leather, and brine.

The gun deck was nearly completely submerged as Jim and Matilda propelled themselves through the gun ports and out into the open water.

Jim grabbed Matilda's hand, and they kicked for the surface, swimming as fast as they could so they wouldn't be sucked to the bottom of the sea with the *Black Rat* and her scurvy crew.

15.
SUNRISE

The water was cold. But Jim and Matilda could make out the headlights of the amphibious vehicle motoring towards them. They clung to some flotsam as the *Black Rat* finally disappeared beneath the waves.

"Woof!" barked Bones from the rowboat, which was drifting in the dark, piled high with the stolen treasures from the Dull-on-Sea Museum.

The vehicle came to a splashy stop, and Jim's dad pulled Jim and Matilda, dripping wet, on board. He wrapped them in blankets and secured a tow for the rowboat.

"ARRR! That all worked out fine, eh, kids?" said Jim's dad. "We'd have been 'ere sooner, but those maggots locked us up in our own food store. It'd have been hell without them chocolate-chip cookies. . . . Let's get back to the *Blackhole* an' get y'all warm and dry."

A few hours later, as the sun rose, the Jolley-Rogers and Matilda were motoring toward the shore, towing the booty-laden rowboat through the gentle swell.

"It'd be best ye don't tell yer parents about this little adventure, Matilda," said Jim's mom. "They might not let ye come and play again."

Jim's dad had already phoned the Dull-on-Sea police, and Chief Inspector Klewless was waiting at the harbor with several of his officers and a van. It was early morning, so there weren't many other people around.

A few bemused fishermen watched and a seagull cackled as the vehicle emerged from the water, dripping with seaweed, water pouring from its bilges. The Jolley-Rogers unhitched the rowboat, and Jim's dad shook the dumbstruck Chief Inspector's hand.

"Righto, here's yer treasure, then, Cap'n Klewless," said Jim's dad. "It should all be there, give or take a cutlass or two. Those ghostly pirates shouldn't be botherin' ye again either. We've taken care of 'em for ye, with the help of brave Matilda 'ere. Oh, and sorry about the smell. I've been guttin' kippers for breakfast. Well . . . Best be off, then. . . . Cheerio!'

"Time to get ye home, Tilly," said Jim Lad.

They all climbed back into the vehicle and trundled off to Matilda's house.

"GOOD MORNIN', me hearties!" shouted Jim's dad.

Matilda's mom and dad stood in the doorway, rubbing their eyes. It was five thirty on a Sunday morning, and they hadn't expected Matilda to arrive home quite so early. They had hoped they would get to sleep late and be able to read the paper in bed.

"I hope it ain't too early for yers!" boomed Jim's dad. "But we've got lots to do. Y'know, swabbin' the decks 'n' all that stuff. Matilda's a bit tired, so we brought her back in her jim-jams."

Matilda appeared behind him in her pajamas, clutching a plastic bag full of wet clothes.

"See you soon, Jim," said Matilda, giving him a hug. "And thanks for everything!" she said quietly into his ear.

"'Bye, Tilly. Remember to write me notes!" replied Jim.

"I will," said Matilda as she waved good-bye to the Jolley-Rogers and returned to her ordinary life.

"Until next time . . ." she whispered.

The JOLLEY-ROGERS'
GUIDE TO PIRATE-SPEAK

AVAST AND BELAY! — Sea-dog speak for "Stop and tie up your ship!" If a cap'n should say it to you, you'd better listen, and fast.

BILGE — The lowest part of your vessel, where stinking water collects. Don't forget your boots. . . .

BILGE RAT — A pirate insult. Save this one for those stinking, scurvy sea dogs you really don't like.

BLOW MY SCUTTLEBUTT — polite landlubbers might say, "Well, I never," but this is *a lot* ruder. And a lot more fun.

BOWSPRIT — The pointy bit that sticks out at the front of a ship. Good for spearing sea monsters and hanging your laundry on.

CURMUDGEON — "Grumpy old thing." Careful who you say it to. Especially if they *are* old.

FLOTSAM — Bits of shipwreck you'll spot floating in the sea or washed up on the beach. Makes lovely ornaments. Or furniture.

FO'C'SLE — From "forecastle," The part of the ship where the scurviest of seafarers bed down at night. Also home to the anchor chains and the barnacles that cling to them.

GANGPLANK — A plank of wood to walk on to get from shore to ship. Or to walk *off*, into the deep blue sea, if you've been a very naughty pirate.

GIZZARDS — A *much* funnier word for your innards than *stomach* or *tummy*. See if you can drop it into conversation.

GROG — A grown-up pirate's favorite drink. It'll probably make him fall asleep. Or sing a sea chantey.

IF THAT'S THE CUT OF YER JIB — Pirate speak for "If that's your style."

KEELHAULING — A nasty pirate punishment. You'll be dunked in the sea and dragged across the barnacle-crusted keel. Ouch.

LANDLUBBER — Someone who lives on land and doesn't really understand life on the scurvy seas. It's just a teensy bit rude.

LEEWARD SIDE — The side of the ship facing away from the wind. The side you want to be on if you've forgotten your coat.

PARLEY — Have a chitchat to end an argument instead of having a fight. Although usually pirates are too grumpy for chitchats and prefer a good old fight.

POOP DECK — *Not* what it sounds like. The deck at the back of a ship that's higher than the other decks. Mainly so the cap'n can stand up there and feel important.

SCUGS — A pirate insult.

SKULKS — Another pirate insult.

SQUABS — *Another* pirate insult. Pirates are really good at inventing them. . . .

SWABBIN' THE DECKS — Cleaning the ship's deck, a job reserved for those pirates who probably sleep in the fo's'cle, when they've finished cleaning the anchor chains.

Don't miss Jim Lad and Matilda's
other swashbuckling adventure!

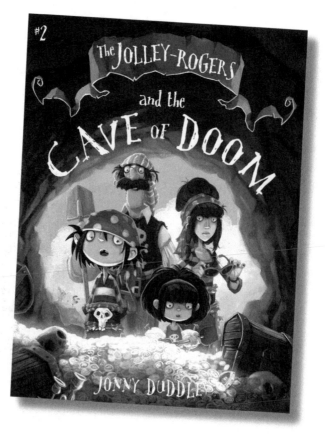

Available in paperback and as an e-book

AHOY THERE!

Here be more treasures from Jonny Duddle:

Available in hardcover

JONNY DUDDLE is the author-illustrator of several picture books, including *The Pirate-Cruncher*, *The King of Space*, *Gigantosaurus*, and *The Pirates Next Door*, which introduced readers to Matilda and the Jolley-Rogers family. He was also an animator for the movie *The Pirates! Band of Misfits* and illustrated the covers for the reissued Harry Potter books. He lives in the wet and windy hills of north Wales, where he spends most of his time drawing and busily creating worlds, sprawled across his studio floor, with paper everywhere.